Elly Rose

IN DENMARK

Maggie O

All photos used to create the images were taken by Maggie O

Acknowlegement to Rebecca McMeen
for use of her Berkley Doll to create Elly Rose

Printed in Australia 2018

ISBN 978-0-6480513-7-4 Paperback

Published by Elly Rose Publishing
Townsville, QLD, 4814
www.ellyrosetownsville.com.au

*For my daughters Caitlin and Sophie
who travelled to Denmark with me when
they were young*

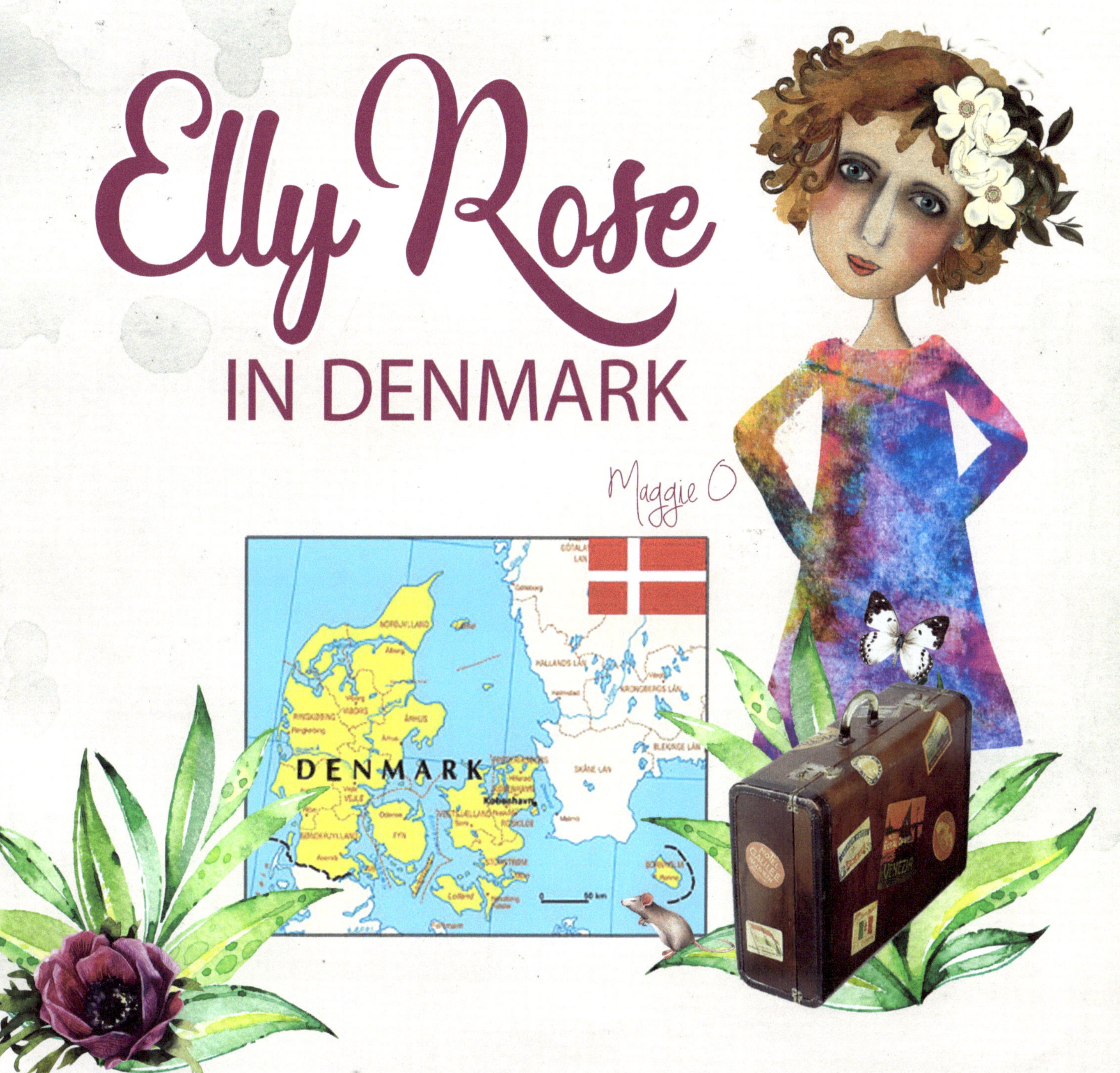

Elly Rose

IN DENMARK

Maggie O

"Something smells good," said Elly Rose as they
walked past a hot dog stand.

Aunty Nete ordered two hot dogs with
crispy onions and sauce.

"Yum! This is the best hot dog ever," said
Elly Rose as they continued walking.

Elly Rose loved the colours of the houses
along the canal in Nyhavn.

"The houses are so petty," Elly Rose said.

"They were built a long time ago,"
said Aunty Nete.

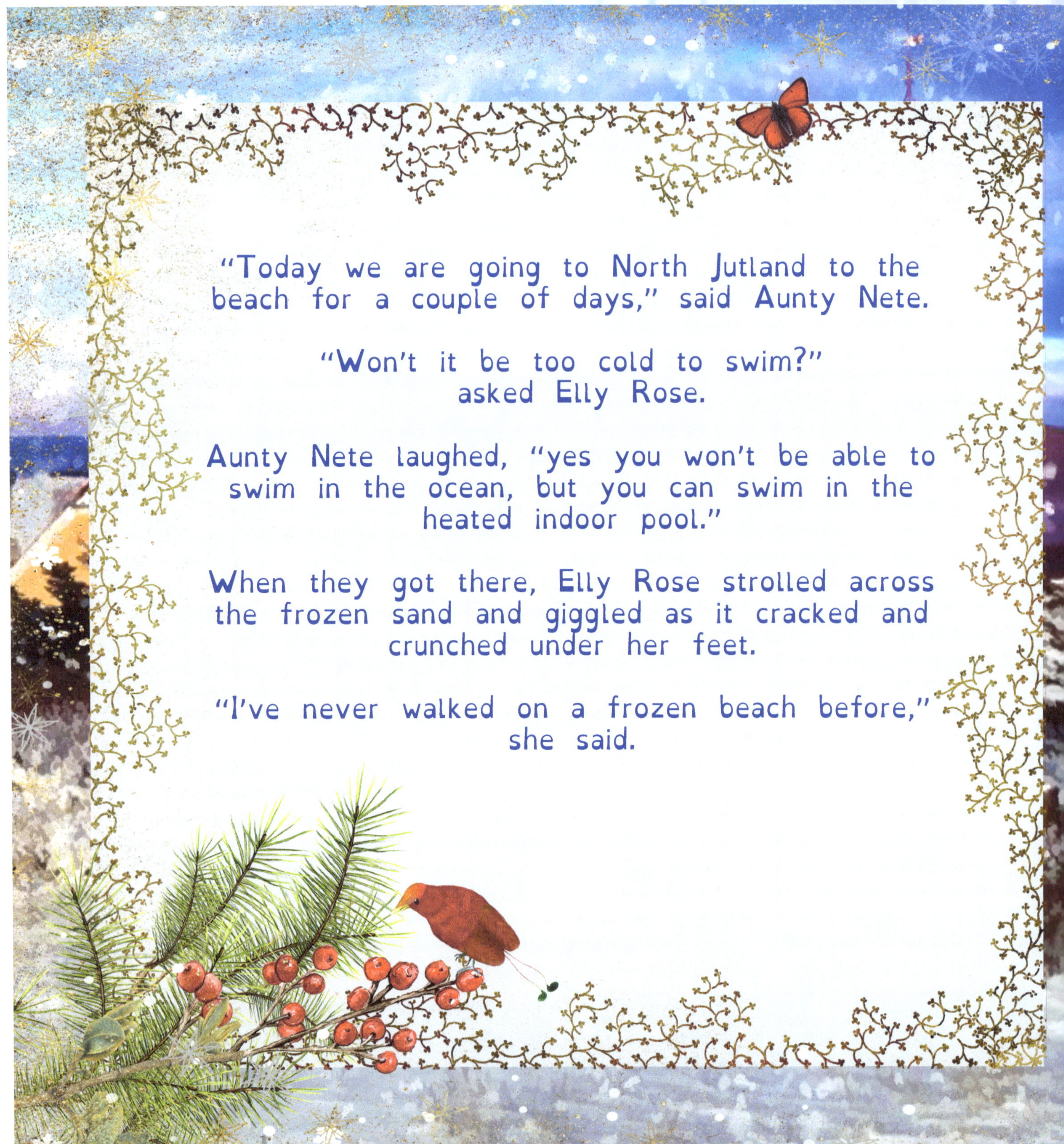

"Today we are going to North Jutland to the beach for a couple of days," said Aunty Nete.

"Won't it be too cold to swim?"
asked Elly Rose.

Aunty Nete laughed, "yes you won't be able to swim in the ocean, but you can swim in the heated indoor pool."

When they got there, Elly Rose strolled across the frozen sand and giggled as it cracked and crunched under her feet.

"I've never walked on a frozen beach before,"
she said.

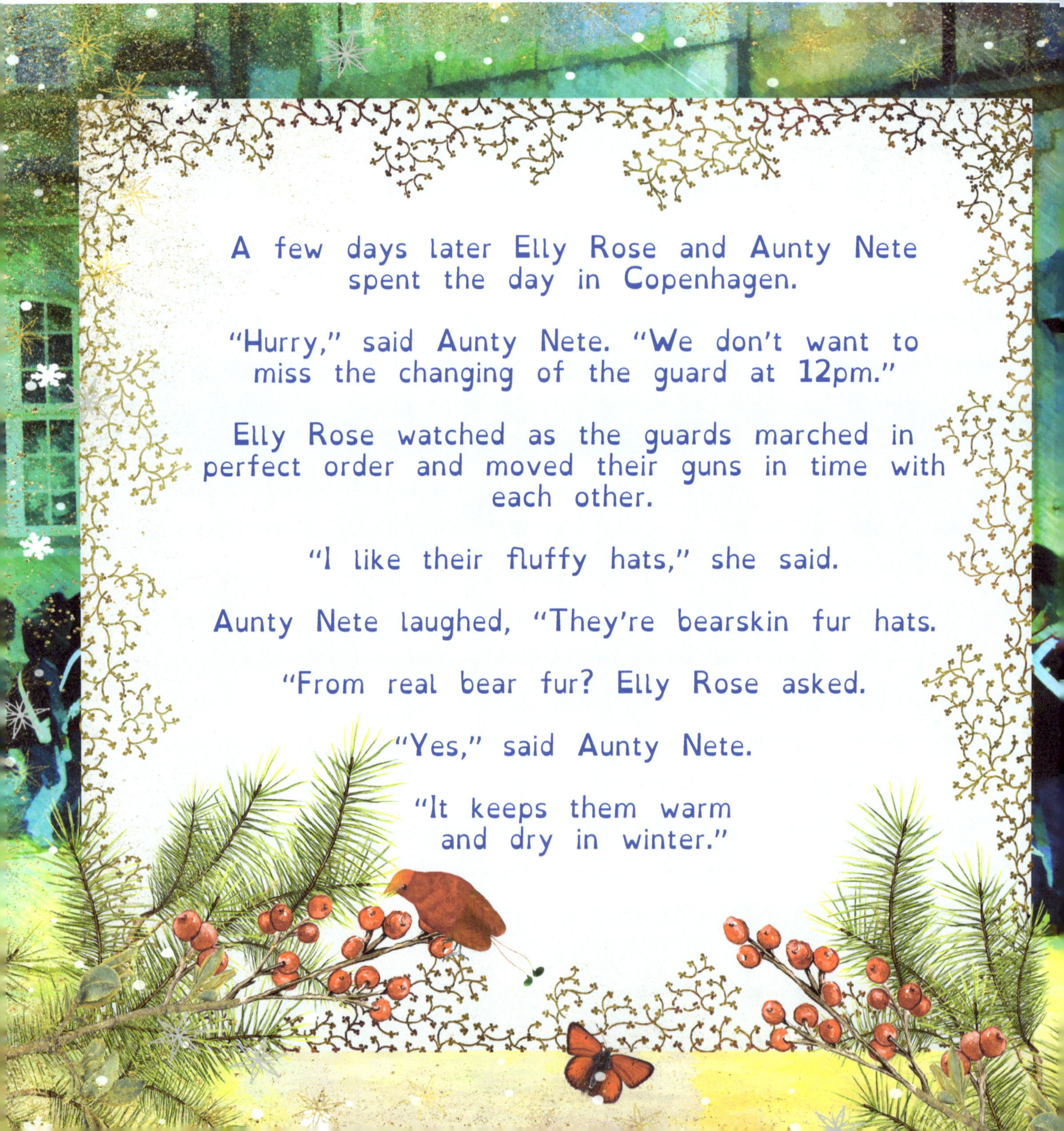

A few days later Elly Rose and Aunty Nete spent the day in Copenhagen.

"Hurry," said Aunty Nete. "We don't want to miss the changing of the guard at 12pm."

Elly Rose watched as the guards marched in perfect order and moved their guns in time with each other.

"I like their fluffy hats," she said.

Aunty Nete laughed, "They're bearskin fur hats.

"From real bear fur? Elly Rose asked.

"Yes," said Aunty Nete.

"It keeps them warm and dry in winter."

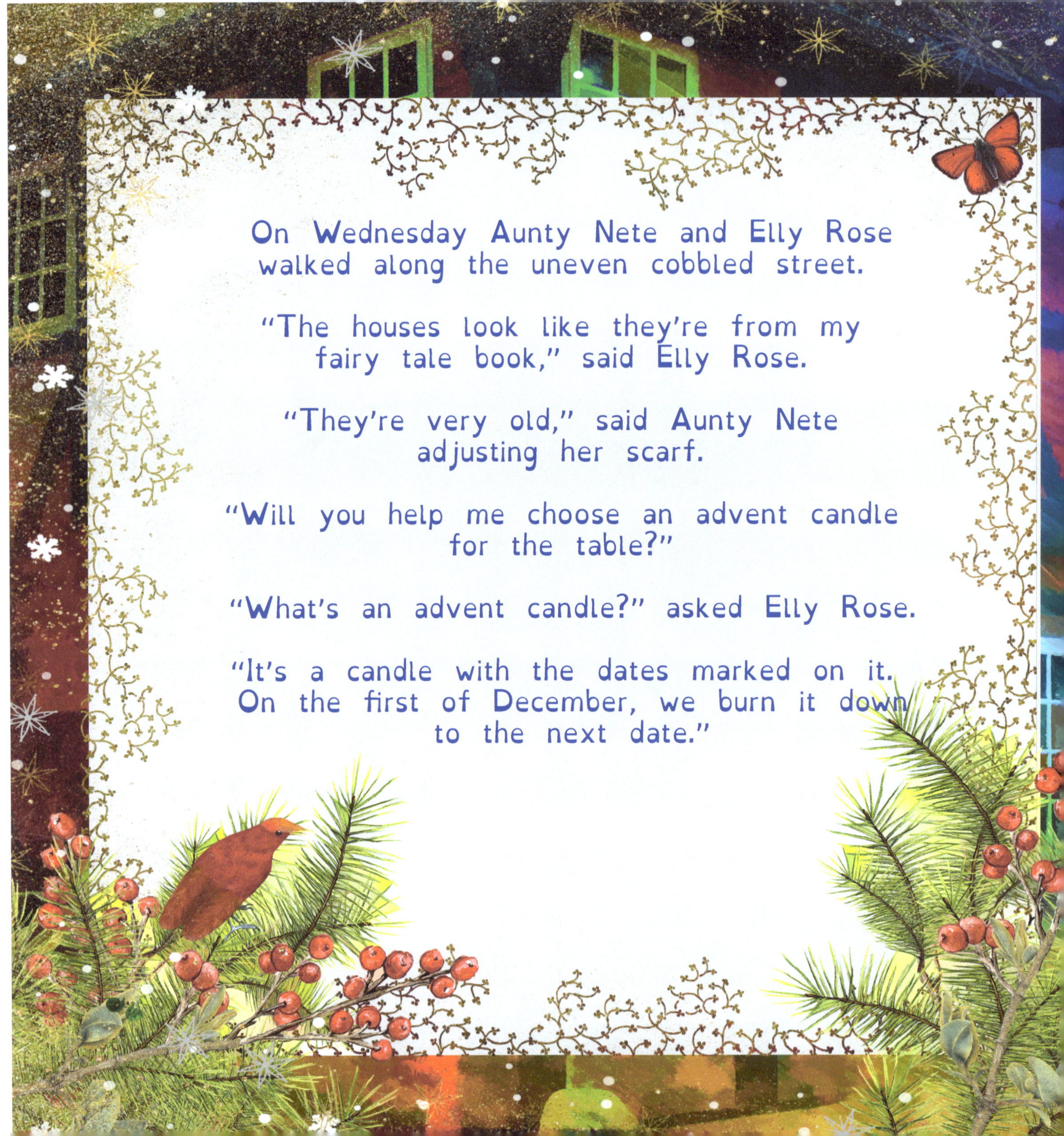

On Wednesday Aunty Nete and Elly Rose walked along the uneven cobbled street.

"The houses look like they're from my fairy tale book," said Elly Rose.

"They're very old," said Aunty Nete adjusting her scarf.

"Will you help me choose an advent candle for the table?"

"What's an advent candle?" asked Elly Rose.

"It's a candle with the dates marked on it. On the first of December, we burn it down to the next date."

Erik den Røde

Thursday evening Elly Rose and Aunty Nete
walked through the gates of Tivoli Gardens.

Elly Rose stared at the pretty lights and
Christmas decorations.

"It's the most beautiful place I've seen,"
Elly Rose said forgetting how cold
she had felt moments earlier.

"Tivoli Gardens is magical at this time of year.
We visit every December," said Aunty Nete.

Aunty Nete handed Elly Rose
a cup of hot chocolate.

"Drink this it will keep you
warm," she said.

TIVOLI
JUL I TIVOLI

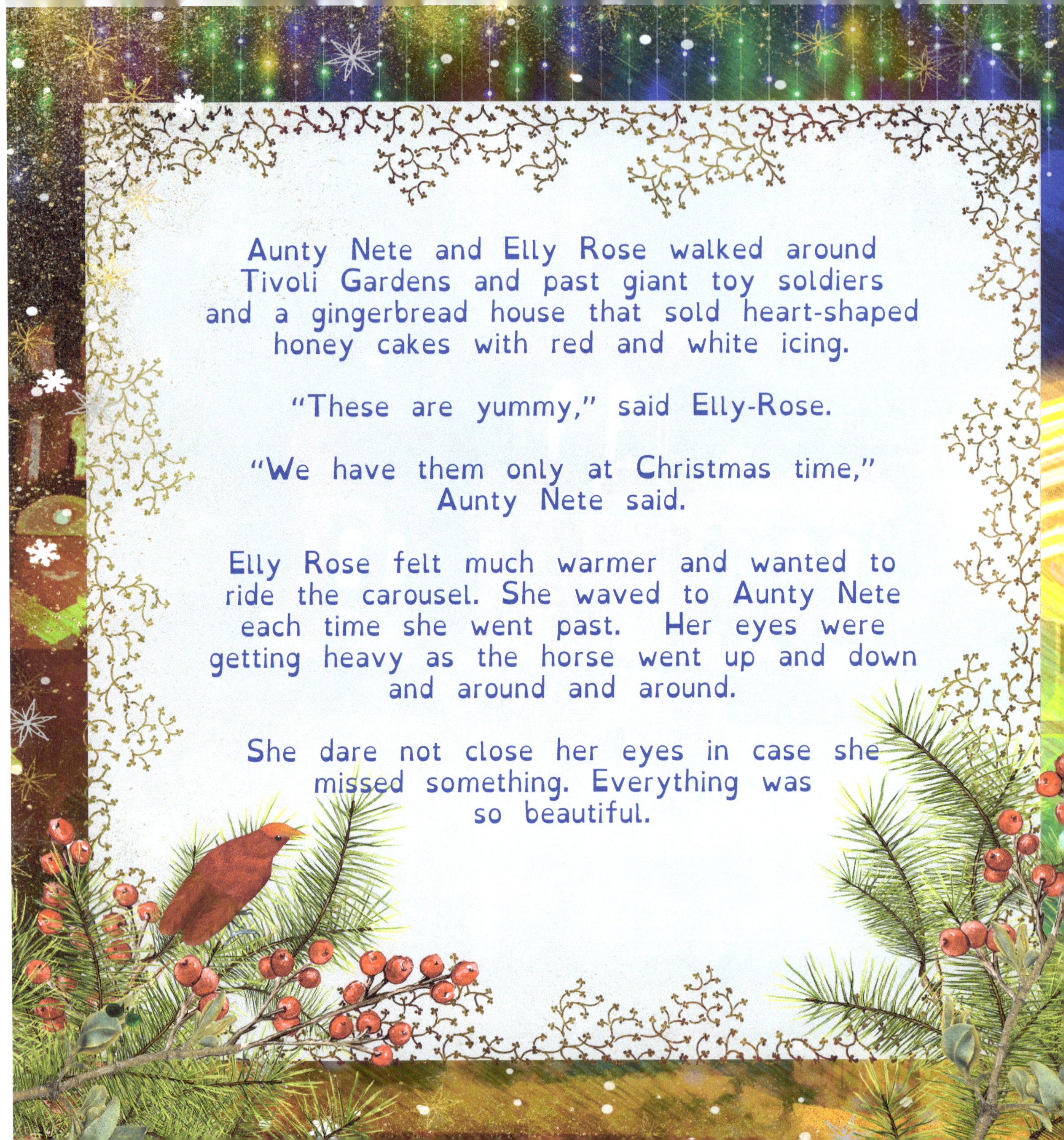

Aunty Nete and Elly Rose walked around
Tivoli Gardens and past giant toy soldiers
and a gingerbread house that sold heart-shaped
honey cakes with red and white icing.

"These are yummy," said Elly-Rose.

"We have them only at Christmas time,"
Aunty Nete said.

Elly Rose felt much warmer and wanted to
ride the carousel. She waved to Aunty Nete
each time she went past. Her eyes were
getting heavy as the horse went up and down
and around and around.

She dare not close her eyes in case she
missed something. Everything was
so beautiful.

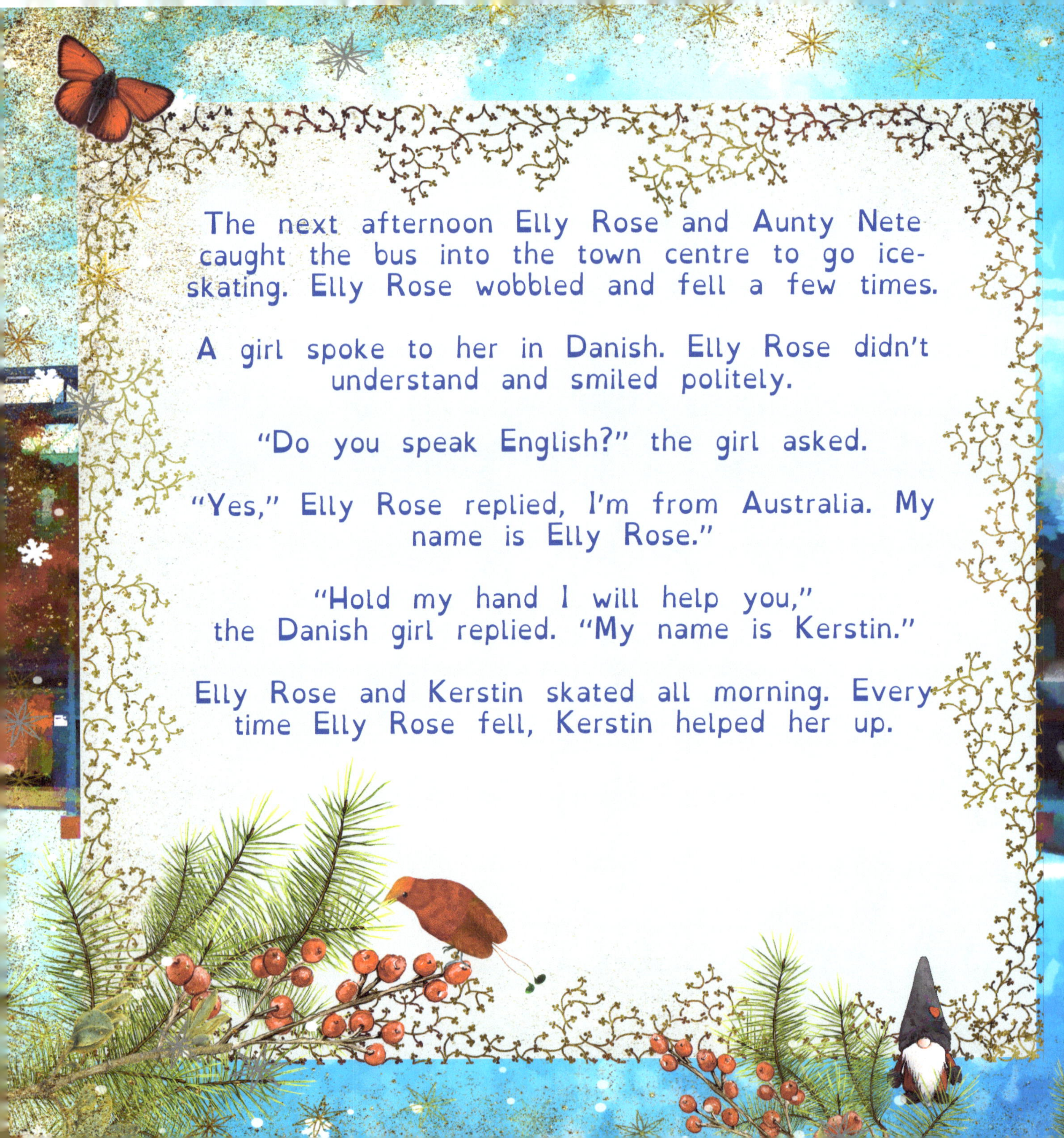

The next afternoon Elly Rose and Aunty Nete caught the bus into the town centre to go ice-skating. Elly Rose wobbled and fell a few times.

A girl spoke to her in Danish. Elly Rose didn't understand and smiled politely.

"Do you speak English?" the girl asked.

"Yes," Elly Rose replied, I'm from Australia. My name is Elly Rose."

"Hold my hand I will help you," the Danish girl replied. "My name is Kerstin."

Elly Rose and Kerstin skated all morning. Every time Elly Rose fell, Kerstin helped her up.

A few days later Elly Rose
and Aunty Nete walked past another bakery.

"Let's try a different treat," said Aunty Nete.

"Can I try one of those giant knots please,"
said Elly Rose.

Aunty Nete ordered two bagels.

"There are many yummy treats here,"
said Elly Rose.

"Only at Christmas", reminded Aunty Nete.

Elly Rose removed her gloves and ate her bagel.

"It gets dark so early.
It's only 4pm," said Elly Rose.

Aunty Nete laughed. "Yes, it gets darker
much earlier than North Queensland."

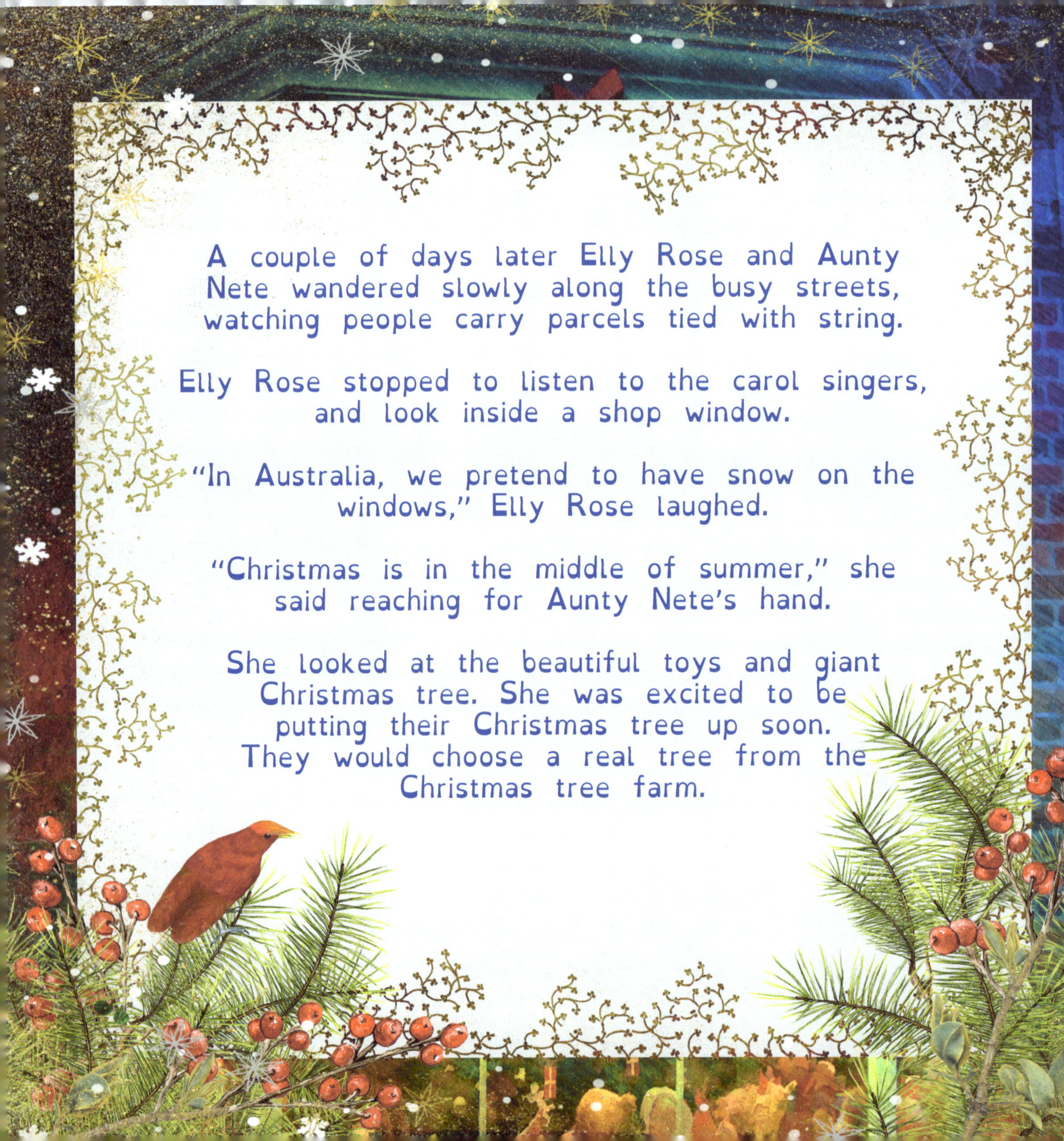

A couple of days later Elly Rose and Aunty Nete wandered slowly along the busy streets, watching people carry parcels tied with string.

Elly Rose stopped to listen to the carol singers, and look inside a shop window.

"In Australia, we pretend to have snow on the windows," Elly Rose laughed.

"Christmas is in the middle of summer," she said reaching for Aunty Nete's hand.

She looked at the beautiful toys and giant Christmas tree. She was excited to be putting their Christmas tree up soon. They would choose a real tree from the Christmas tree farm.

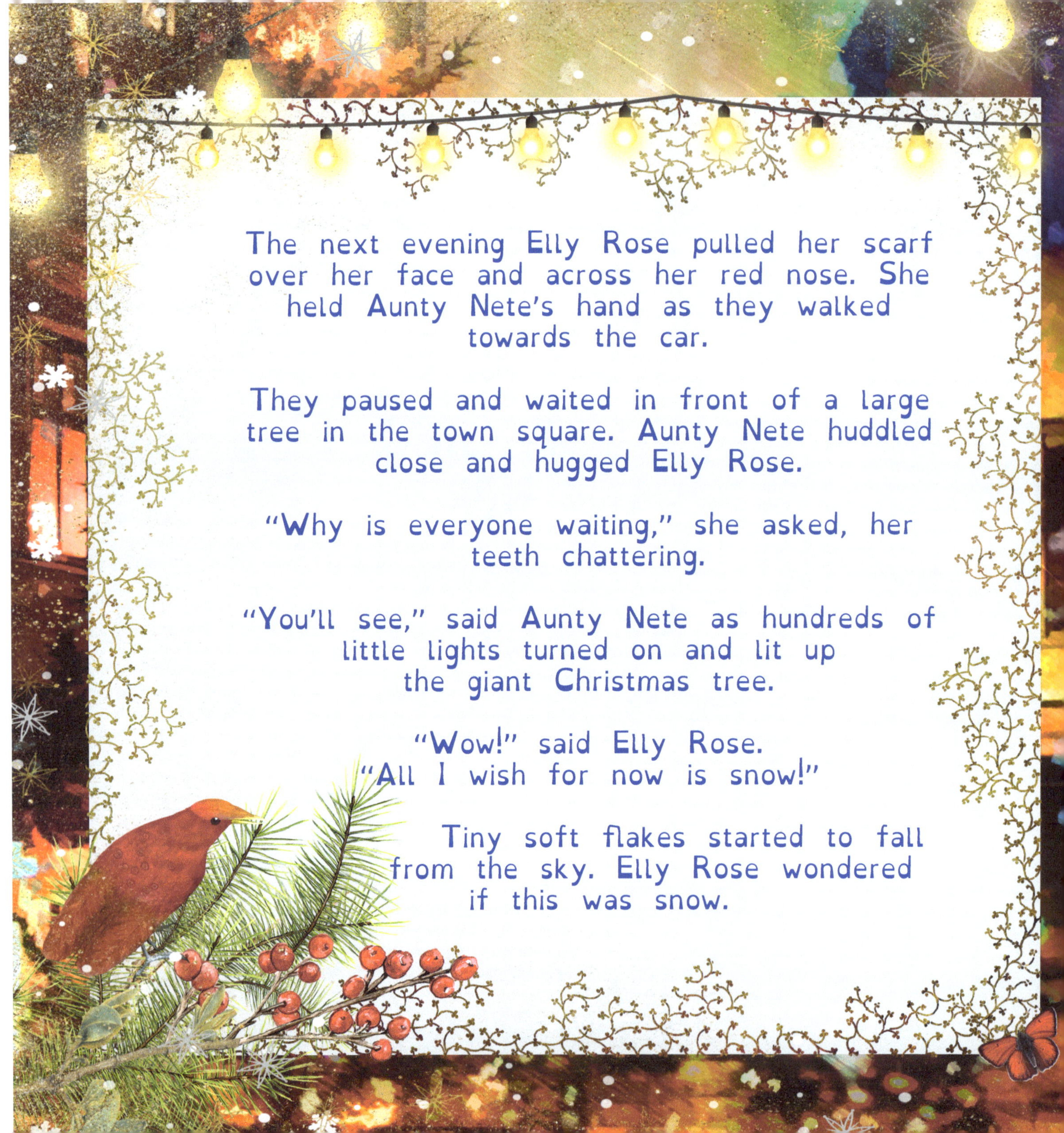

The next evening Elly Rose pulled her scarf over her face and across her red nose. She held Aunty Nete's hand as they walked towards the car.

They paused and waited in front of a large tree in the town square. Aunty Nete huddled close and hugged Elly Rose.

"Why is everyone waiting," she asked, her teeth chattering.

"You'll see," said Aunty Nete as hundreds of little lights turned on and lit up the giant Christmas tree.

"Wow!" said Elly Rose.
"All I wish for now is snow!"

Tiny soft flakes started to fall from the sky. Elly Rose wondered if this was snow.

Elly Rose got up early to help hang the candle wreath and to light the advent candle they had purchased a few weeks ago. She observed as it burned to just below the next date and blew it out.

"Today we will be cooking gingerbread and shortbread," said Aunty Nete.

Elly Rose put on an apron and started measuring out the ingredients.

"I like the smell of the cinnamon," she said.

"Yes cinnamon smells like Christmas," Aunty Nete said.

They baked all day, placing warm biscuits on the kitchen windowsill to cool.

15
16
17
18
19
20
21
22
23

The next morning Elly Rose couldn't see out the window. Everything was white. She raced downstairs forgetting to brush her hair.

"Wait! You need to get dressed properly before you go outside. It will be cold," said Aunty Nete.

Elly Rose pulled on her clothes, jacket, boots and gloves. She was getting quicker with her gloves.

Today they were choosing their Christmas tree. Elly Rose stomped through the soft snow looking for the perfect Christmas tree.

"How will we get it home?" she asked. "It won't fit in the car."

"We will tie it onto the roof," said Aunty Nete.

Finally, Christmas Eve was here, and it was snowing. Elly Rose raced outside to play with the laughing children.

The pond had frozen overnight. Elly Rose wondered how the birds would get water. She poked a little hole in the ice for them. She watched Aunty Nete hang red apples and little birdhouses in the trees.

"After lunch, we'll go to church and sing Christmas carols," Aunty Nete said.

It was strange hearing her favourite carols sung in Danish. Elly Rose sang proudly in English.

After church, they walked home through the soft snow. The frozen leaves crunching under Elly Roses feet as she walked.

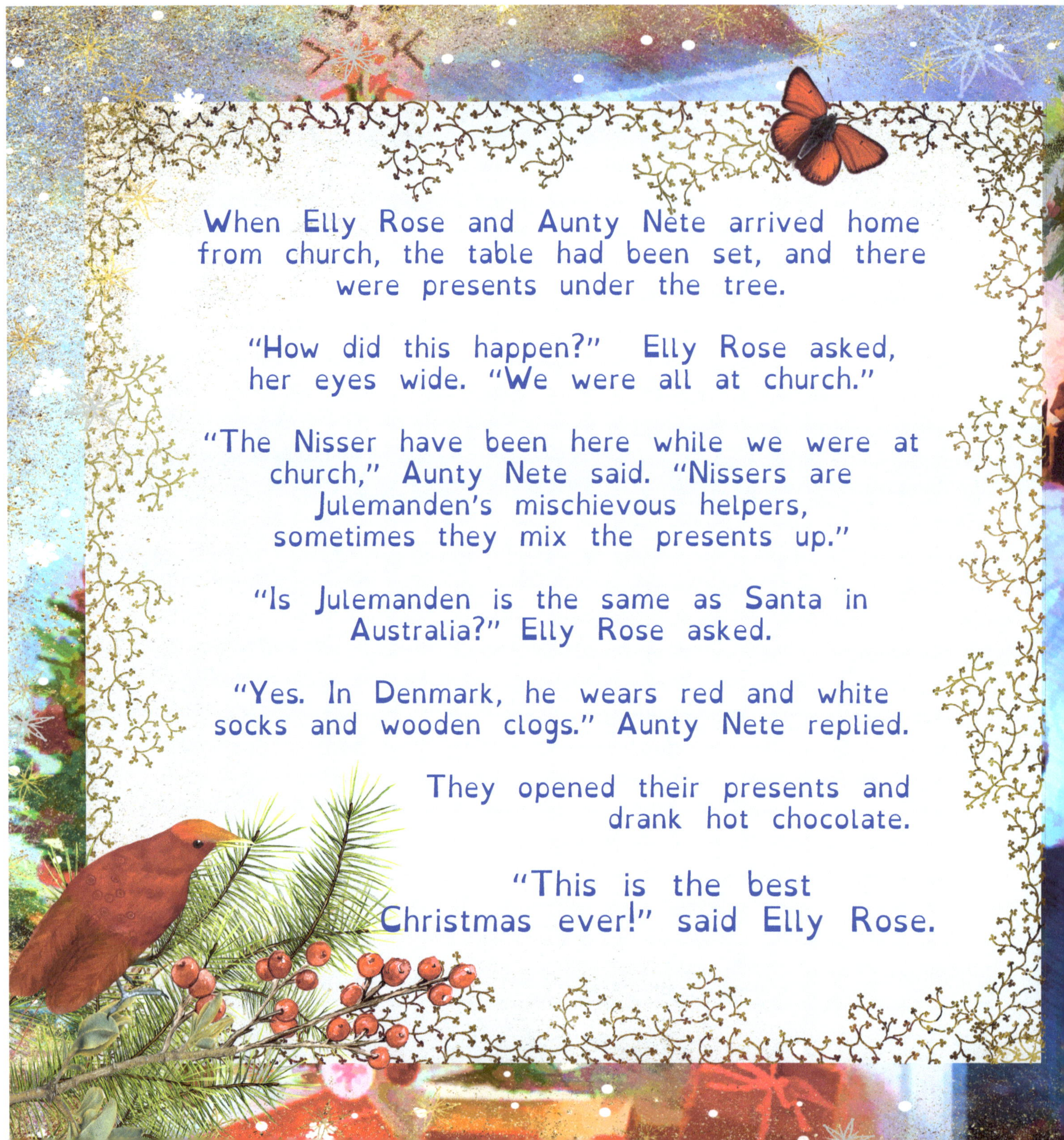

When Elly Rose and Aunty Nete arrived home from church, the table had been set, and there were presents under the tree.

"How did this happen?" Elly Rose asked, her eyes wide. "We were all at church."

"The Nisser have been here while we were at church," Aunty Nete said. "Nissers are Julemanden's mischievous helpers, sometimes they mix the presents up."

"Is Julemanden is the same as Santa in Australia?" Elly Rose asked.

"Yes. In Denmark, he wears red and white socks and wooden clogs." Aunty Nete replied.

They opened their presents and drank hot chocolate.

"This is the best Christmas ever!" said Elly Rose.

Maggie travelled to Denmark to experience a white Christmas. She enjoyed learning about the Danish Christmas traditions and choosing her own real Christmas tree. She made traditional Christmas decorations and baked Christmas cookies and treats. Maggie also enjoyed the snow and learning to ice skate, and build a snowman.

About the Author - Maggie O

Maggie grew up in Western Queensland in a small town called Julia Creek. She travelled from a young age and has visited many countries. She loves sharing her experiences and stories. Maggie hopes her books will inspire children to embark on their own adventures when they are older. She has travelled overseas with two small children and discovered children love learning why people do things differently.

The illustrations are created from photos Maggie takes while on her adventure. She transforms them into detailed miniature works of art.

The Elly Rose Series

Maggie was inspired to write a travel series for children who may not have the opportunity to travel. Elly Rose experiences many different cultures, both in Australia and overseas.

The fonts and colours used in this book assist reluctant readers or children with dyslexia to enjoy reading.

Did you find Elly Rose's travelling companion?

Miss Marmalade, an Australian mouse that travels with Elly Rose on every adventure. She is hidden in the pages of this book.

Also joining her on this adventure, is a nisser and red butterflies.

Some fun Danish words to learn.

Hej	Hello
Farvel	Goodbye
Tak	Thanks
Vaer venlig	Please
Jeg er Sulten	I'm hungry
Jul	Christmas

DID YOU KNOW?

Denmark can fit into Australia approximately **180** times.

Julemanden is similar to Santa Clauss and wears wooden clog shoes.

Nisser are Julemanden's helpers that get into mischief all the time. Traditionaly they have a long white beard and wear a knitted cap. They look similar to a garden gnome.

Risalamande (cold rice pudding) is served on Christmas eve. There is a whole almond hidden in the dessert and whoever gets the almond wins a present.

Danish people open their presents on Christmas Eve.

www.ingramcontent.com/pod-product-compliance
Lightning Source LLC
Chambersburg PA
CBHW041130100726
47911CB00002B/92